Smriti Prasadam-Halls   Alison Brown

I Love You Night and Day

BLOOMSBURY

LONDON NEW DELHI NEW YORK SYDNEY

I love you most, I love you best,
Much, much more than all the rest.

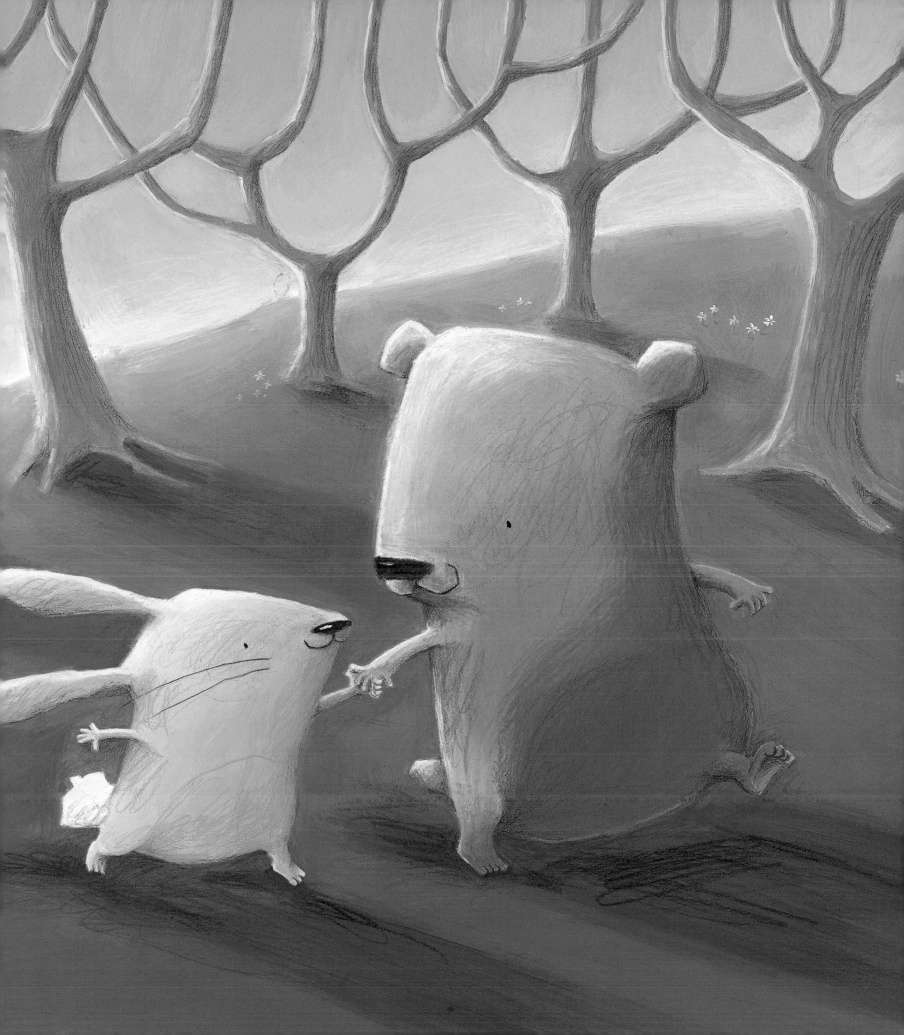

I love you tall, I love you high,

Way up in the sunny sky.

I love you far, I love you wide,

From over here . . .

to the other side.

I love you low, I love you deep,
Down where the octopuses sleep.

I love you huge, I love you vast,
For the fun to come and the fun that's passed.

I love you big, I love you tough,
When the path is smooth and when it's rough.

I love you strong, I love you small,
Together we have it all.

I love you wild, I love you loud,
I shout it out and I feel proud.

I love you soft, I love you still,

And you know I always will.

I love you close, I love you tight,

When you're wrong . . . and when you're right.

I love you night, I love you day,
In every moment, come what may . . .

... Because I love you with my whole heart,

From where you end . . . to where you start.

For Mum ~ Aama, we love you most, we love you best,
we love you to bits . . . to crumbs . . . to cinnamon tea
~ S.P-H. & the boys

To my Mum and Dad ~ A.B.

Bloomsbury Publishing, London, New Delhi, New York and Sydney

First published in Great Britain in 2014 by Bloomsbury Publishing Plc
50 Bedford Square, London, WC1B 3DP

Text copyright © Smriti Prasadam-Halls 2014
Inspired by Ephesians 3:17-19
Illustration copyright © Alison Brown 2014
The moral rights of the author and illustrator have been asserted

A CIP catalogue record for this book is available from the British Library

ISBN 978 1 4088 3972 0 (HB)
ISBN 978 1 4088 3973 7 (PB)
ISBN 978 1 4088 3971 3 (eBook)

Printed in China by C & C Offset Printing Co Ltd, Shenzhen, Guangdong

1 3 5 7 9 10 8 6 4 2

www.bloomsbury.com